NINE-IN-ONE GRR! GRR!

A folktale from the Hmong people of Laos

Told by Blia Xiong ✜ Adapted by Cathy Spagnoli ✜ Illustrated by Nancy Hom

CHILDREN'S BOOK PRESS
San Francisco, California

Many years ago when the earth was nearer the sky than it is today, there lived the first tiger. She and her mate had no babies and so the lonely tiger often thought about the future, wondering how many cubs she would have.

iger decided to visit the great god Shao, who lived in the sky, who was kind and gentle and knew everything. Surely Shao could tell her how many cubs she would have.

Tiger set out on the road that led to the sky. She climbed through forests of striped bamboo and wild banana trees, past plants curved like rooster tail feathers, and over rocks shaped like sleeping dragons.

4

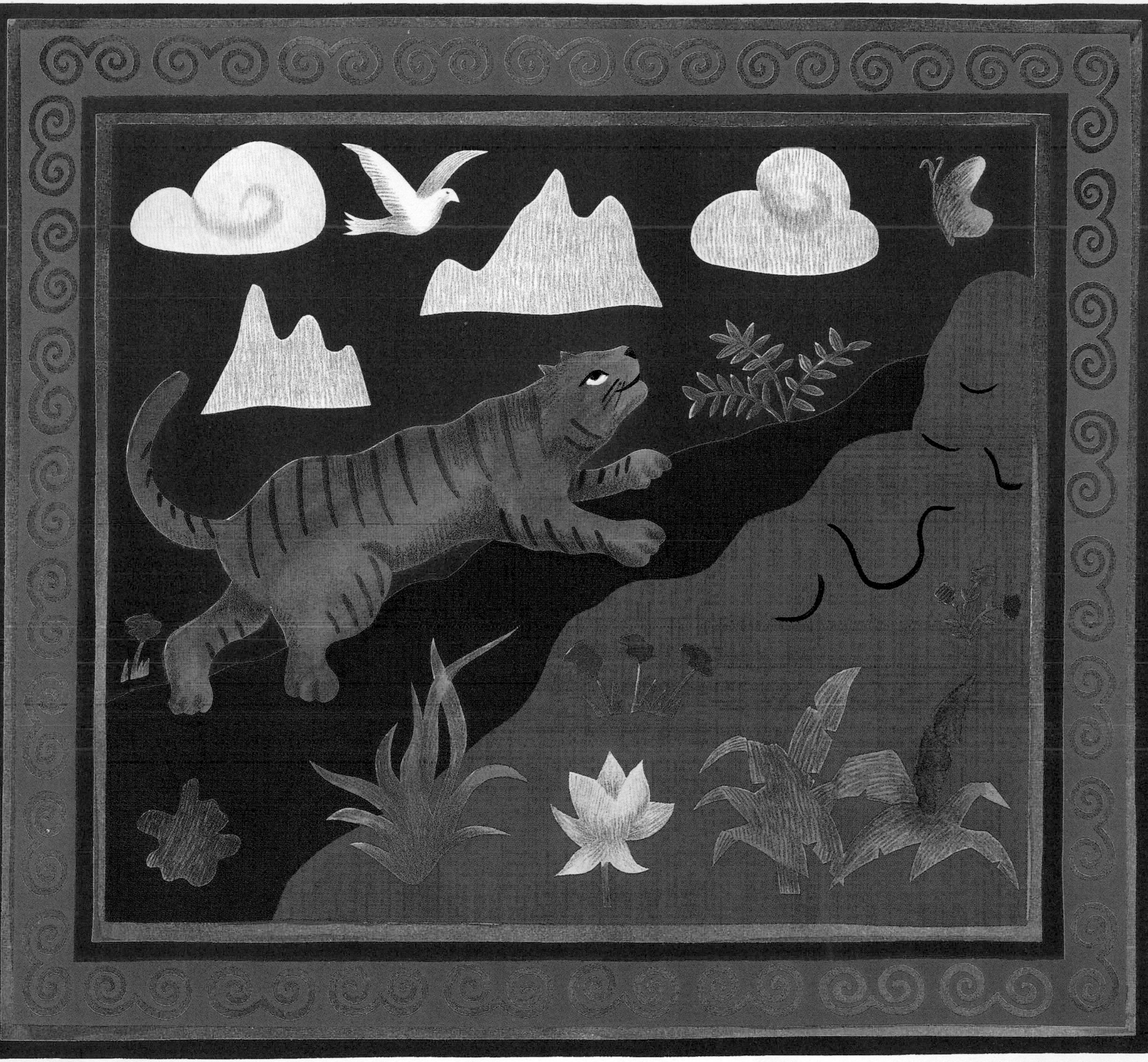

t last Tiger came to a stone wall. Beyond the wall was a garden where children played happily under a plum tree. A large house stood nearby, its colorful decorations shining in the sun. This was the land of the great Shao, a peaceful land without sickness or death.

hao himself came out to greet Tiger. The silver coins dangling from his belt sounded softly as he walked.

"Why did you come here, Tiger?" he asked gently.

"O great Shao," answered Tiger respectfully, "I am lonely and want to know how many cubs I will have."

hao was silent for a moment. Then he replied, "Nine each year."

"How wonderful," purred Tiger. "Thank you so much, great Shao." And she turned to leave with her good news.

"One moment, Tiger," said Shao. "You must remember carefully what I said. The words alone tell you how many cubs you will have. Do not forget them, for if you do, I cannot help you."

At first Tiger was happy as she followed the road back to earth. But soon, she began to worry.

"Oh dear," she said to herself. "My memory is so bad. How will I ever remember those important words of Shao?" She thought and she thought. At last, she had an idea. "I'll make up a little song to sing. Then I won't forget." So Tiger began to sing:

Nine-in-one, Grr! Grr!
Nine-in-one, Grr! Grr!

Down the mountain went Tiger, past the rocks shaped like sleeping dragons, past the plants curved like rooster tail feathers, through the forests of striped bamboo and wild banana trees. Over and over she sang her song:

Nine-in-one, Grr! Grr!
Nine-in-one, Grr! Grr!

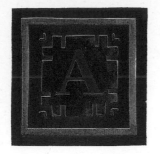s Tiger came closer to her cave, she passed through clouds of tiny white butterflies. She heard monkeys and barking deer. She saw green-striped snakes, quails and pheasants. None of the animals listened to her song—except one big, clever, black bird, the Eu bird.

"Hmm," said Bird to herself. "I wonder why Tiger is coming down the mountain singing that song and grinning from ear to ear. I'd better find out." So Bird soared up the ladder which was a shortcut to Shao's home.

wise Shao," asked Bird politely,
"why is Tiger singing over and over:

Nine-in-one, Grr! Grr!
Nine-in-one, Grr! Grr!

And Shao explained that he had just told
Tiger she would have nine cubs each year.

hat's terrible!" squawked Bird. "If Tiger has nine cubs each year, they will eat all of us. Soon there will be nothing but tigers in the land. You must change what you said, O Shao!"

"I cannot take back my words," sighed Shao. "I promised Tiger that she would have nine cubs every year as long as she remembered my words."

"As long as she remembered your words," repeated Bird thoughtfully. "Then I know what I must do, O great Shao."

Bird now had a plan. She could
hardly wait to try it out. Quickly,
she returned to earth in search of Tiger.

Bird reached her favorite tree as old grandmother sun was setting, just in time to hear Tiger coming closer and closer and still singing:

Nine-in-one, Grr! Grr!
Nine-in-one, Grr! Grr!

Tiger was concentrating so hard on her song that she didn't even see Bird landing in the tree above her.

uddenly, Bird began to flap her wings furiously. "Flap! Flap! Flap!" went Bird's big, black wings.

"Who's that?" cried Tiger.

"It's only me," answered Bird innocently.

Tiger looked up and growled at Bird: "Grr! Grr! Bird. You made me forget my song with all your noise."

h, I can help you," chirped Bird sweetly. I heard you walking through the woods. You were singing:

One-in-nine, Grr! Grr!
One-in-nine, Grr! Grr!

"Oh, thank you, thank you, Bird!" cried Tiger. "I will have one cub every nine years. How wonderful! This time I won't forget!"

o Tiger returned to her cave, singing happily:

One-in-nine, Grr! Grr!
One-in-nine, Grr! Grr!

And that is why, the Hmong people say, we don't have too many tigers on the earth today!

ABOUT THE STORY

Blia Xiong heard *Nine-in-One, Grr! Grr!* when she was a small child living in the mountains of Laos.

Blia was one of the first Hmong (pronounced "Mong") to come to Seattle in 1976, fleeing a war that had killed many of her people in Laos. She quickly learned English and helped the many Hmong families who followed from the refugee camps in Thailand. Adapting to a very different lifestyle here was hard for many, especially the elders who missed their old life in Laos. Many Hmong families also felt new tensions as their children grew up here as Asian-Americans in a very different social climate. So, in 1978, Blia helped form a Hmong Association to preserve traditional music, dance, crafts and stories.

Cathy Spagnoli, a professional storyteller in Seattle, started to collect stories from Southeast Asian refugees in 1983 as a way to build cross-cultural bridges. She met Blia and heard *Nine-in-One, Grr! Grr!* at that time. Cathy and Blia are now working on a tape of tales by an elder Hmong storyteller.

Needlework has always been treasured by the Hmong, and since the war a new form of narrative stitchery, the story cloth, has emerged. The illustrations by Nancy Hom are adapted from this technique of colorful multi-imaged embroidery.

Artist Nancy Hom has been creating stunning works of silkscreen art in San Francisco for over fifteen years. Her medium for this book is silkscreen, watercolor and colored pencil. She has illustrated several books for children including *Little Weaver of Thai-Yen Village,* also published by Children's Book Press.

Text copyright © 1989 by Cathy Spagnoli. All rights reserved. Illustrations copyright ©1989 by Nancy Hom. All rights reserved. Design: Nancy Hom. Typesetting: Metro Type. Printed in China through Marwin Productions. Children's Book Press is a nonprofit community publisher.

Library of Congress Cataloging-in-Publication Data
Blia Xiong.
   Nine-in-one, Grr! Grr!
   Summary: When the great god Shao promises Tiger nine cubs each year, Bird comes up with a clever trick to prevent the land from being overrun by tigers.
   [1. Folklore—Laos. 2. Tigers—Folklore] I. Hom, Nancy, ill. II. Spagnoli, Cathy. III. Title.
PZ8.1.B584Ni   1989   398.24'52'09594   89-9891